contemplation

CONTEM

TWISTED SPOON PRESS
Prague

FRANZ KAFKA

PLATION

translated by
KEVIN BLAHUT

illustrated by
FEDELE SPADAFORA

ISBN 80-902171-5-x

Contents

contemplation

CHILDREN ON THE COUNTRY ROAD

I HEARD THE WAGONS driving past the garden fence, and sometimes I saw them through the weakly moving gaps in the foliage. How the wood in their shafts and spokes creaked in the hot summer! Workers came from the fields and laughed that it was a disgrace.

I was sitting on our small swing, resting between the trees in my parents' garden.

In front of the fence it did not stop. Running children were past in an instant; grain wagons with men and women on the sheaves and around them darkened the flowerbeds; near evening I saw a man with a cane walking slowly; a few girls, who approached him arm in arm, stepped into the grass by the side while greeting him.

The birds ascended as though sparkling; I followed them with my glances and saw how they rose with one breath, until I no longer believed they were rising, but that I was falling, and, holding the ropes firmly, I began to swing a little from weakness. Soon I was swinging harder as the wind blew cooler, and trembling stars appeared instead of flying birds.

I received my dinner by candlelight. Often I had both arms on the wooden board and was already tired when I bit into my bread and butter. The curtains, broken through powerfully, billowed in the warm wind, and from time to time someone who was walking by held them in his hands when he wanted to see me better and speak with me. Usually the candle went out soon, and in its dark smoke the gnats that had gathered continued to circle for a while. If someone asked me something from the window, I looked at him as though I were looking into the mountains or into thin air, and an answer did not mean very much to him either.

When someone jumped over the windowsill and reported that the others were already in front of the house, I rose, sighing.

»Why are you sighing like that? What happened? Is it a special misfortune, one that can never be made good? Will we ever be able to recover from it? Is all really lost?«

Nothing was lost. We ran in front of the house.

»Thank God, you're finally here!« — »You always come too late!« — »Why me?« — »I mean you, stay at home if you don't want to come along.« — »No mercy!« — »What? No mercy? What are you talking about?«

We broke through the evening with our heads. There was no day and no night. Soon the buttons of our vests were rubbing together like teeth; soon we were running, the distances between us remaining constant, fire in our mouths, like animals in the tropics. Like curassiers in ancient wars, stamping and high in the air, we forced each other down the short street, and with this momentum in our legs we continued up the country road. A few stepped into the ditches, and scarcely had they disappeared before the dark embankment than they were standing up on the path and looking down at us like strangers.

»Come down!« — »Come up first!« — »Just so you can push us down? We're not that stupid.« — »But you are that cowardly, is that what you're saying? Come on!« — »Really? You? You're the ones who'll push us down? What do you look like?«

We made our attack, were pushed in our chests, and collapsed on the grass of the ditch, falling of our own free will. Everything was warmed equally, in the grass we felt neither warmth nor cold, one only became tired.

If you turned to your right side and put your hand under your ear, then you wanted to fall asleep. Of course you wanted to get up again with a raised chin, but only to fall into a deeper ditch. Then, holding your arm crossed in front, your legs crooked, you wanted to throw yourself against the air and fall into a ditch that was even deeper. And you never wanted to stop.

You hardly thought about how you would finally stretch yourself out to your full length in the last ditch, especially in the knees, and lay down on your back as though sick, laid down to cry. You blinked when a boy, his elbows at his hips, his soles dark, jumped over us, from the embankment to the road.

You saw that the moon was already quite high up; a mail wagon drove by in its light. A wind rose, and you felt it even in the ditches, and nearby the woods began to rustle. Then being alone was no longer so important.

»Where are you?« — »Come here!« — »All together!« — »Where are you hiding? Enough of this nonsense!« — »Don't you know that the post has already gone by?« — »No! Already gone by?« — »Of course, it went by while you were asleep.« — »I was asleep? You must be joking!« — »Don't bother to deny it, anyone can see just by looking at you.« — »But please.« — »Come on!«

We started running again, this time closer together; many of us extended our hands to each other; because we were going downhill it was impossible to hold one's head high enough. Someone called out an Indian war cry, and in our legs we got a gallop like never before; when we jumped the wind lifted up our hips. Nothing could have stopped us; we had so much momentum that even in overtaking each other we could fold our arms and calmly look around.

We stopped at the bridge over the wild brook;

those who had continued running turned back. The water down below beat against the stones and roots as though it were not already late evening. There was no reason why no one jumped onto the rails of the bridge.

A train emerged from some bushes in the distance. All the compartments were lit, and of course all the glass windows were down. One of us began to sing a popular song, but all of us wanted to sing. We sang much faster than the train was going; we shook our arms because our voices were not enough; our voices got tangled up, and we enjoyed the confusion. When you mix your voice with others, you are captured as though with a fishhook.

So we sang, the woods at our backs, the distant travellers in our ears. In the village the grown-ups were still awake; our mothers were preparing our beds for the night.

It was time. I kissed the person next to me, offered the next three my hand, and began to walk back. No one called to me. At the first crossing, where they could no longer see me, I turned around and followed paths back into the woods. I was heading to the town in the south, of which people in our village say:

»Amazing people live there! Think of it, they never sleep!«

»And why not?«

»Because they don't get tired!«

»And why not?«

»Because they're fools!«

»But don't fools get tired?«

»How could fools get tired!«

THE UNMASKING OF A CONFIDENCE MAN

FINALLY, AT TEN O'CLOCK in the evening, accompanied by a man whom I had known before only casually, but who this time had attached himself to me unexpectedly and had been forcing me to wander the streets with him for two hours, I arrived in front of the distinguished house where I had been invited to a party.

»So!« I said, and clapped my hands in order to signal the absolute necessity of parting. I had already made a few more subtle attempts, and was already quite tired.

»Are you going right up?« he asked. In his mouth I heard a sound like teeth knocking against each other.

»Yes.«

I was invited; I had just told him. But I had been invited to go up, where I would have liked so much to be, and not to remain standing here in front of the gate, looking past this person's ears. And now, in addition, to fall silent with him, as though we had decided on a long pause on this spot. And the houses took part in this silence, as well as the darkness above them, on up to the stars. And the steps of people out walking, out of our range of vision, whose paths no one had any desire to guess, the wind, which pressed itself against the other side of the street again and again, a gramophone, which sang against the closed window of a room, — out of this silence they let themselves be heard, as though it had always belonged to them and always would.

And my companion submitted in his name and — after a smile — also in mine, stretched his right arm upwards along the wall and leaned his face against it, closing his eyes.

But I did not see this smile through to the end, because shame suddenly turned me away. It was only through this smile that I was able to recognize that he was nothing but a confidence man. And I had already been in this city for months and had believed that I knew these confidence men thoroughly; how, at night, they approach us from sidestreets, like innkeepers, their hands stretched out before them; how they sidle around the kiosk where we are standing, as though playing hide-and-seek, and spy on us from behind the curve of the pillar with at least one eye; how, when we become anxious at street crossings, they suddenly stand before us on the edge of our sidewalk! I understood them so well; they had been my first city acquaintances in the small pubs, and I owed to them my first glimpse of an unyielding quality, of which I could now think so little from the world that I began to feel it even in myself. How they continued to stand before you, long after you had run away, when there was nothing more for them to trap! How they did not sit down, did not fall, but continued to look at you with glances that still persuaded, even from a distance! And their methods were always the same: They placed themselves before us as broadly as they could; tried to prevent us from arriving at the place where we were headed; prepared a substitute lodging for us in their own breasts, and if the feeling that had collected in us rebelled, they took it as an embrace and threw themselves into it head first.

And this time I had recognized these old tricks only after having been with this person for so long.

I rubbed my fingertips together in order to undo the disgrace.

My man, however, was still leaning here as before, still thinking he had me fooled, and his satisfaction with his destiny reddened the cheek that was not facing the wall.

»Exposed!« I said, and tapped him softly on the shoulder. Then I hurried up the stairs and into the anteroom, and the faces of the servants, all so groundlessly trusting, cheered me like a beautiful surprise. I looked at all of them in turn while they took my coat and dusted off my boots. Then, straightening myself to my full height, I gave a sigh of relief and entered the hall.

THE SUDDEN WALK

IN THE EVENING, WHEN you seem to have decided once and for all to stay at home, have put on your house jacket, are sitting at the lit table after dinner and have taken up the piece of work or game after the completion of which you usually go to sleep, when the weather outside is unpleasant, which makes staying at home a foregone conclusion, when you have already been sitting at the table for so long that leaving would have to produce general astonishment, when the stairwell is dark and the front door of the building has been locked, and when, despite all this, you rise in a sudden moment of discomfort, change your coat, immediately appear dressed for the street, explain that you have to go, and, after a short goodbye, actually do it, believing, depending on the haste with which you slam the apartment door, to have left more or less agitation behind you, when you find yourself on the street again, with limbs that respond with unusual flexibility to the unexpected freedom you have obtained for them, when, through this one decision you feel all ability to decide gathered within you, when you recognize, with a significance greater than at other times, that you have more strength than you have need to bring about the quickest change easily and to bear it, and you walk down the long streets in this way, — then you have, for the evening, completely stepped outside your family, which veers off into insignificance, while you yourself, quite solid, outlined in black, slapping your thighs, attain your true form.

All of this is intensified even further when you call on a friend at this late hour to see how he is.

DECISIONS

IT SHOULD BE EASY TO lift oneself out of a miserable state with the force of will. I pull myself from the chair, pace around the table, move my head and neck, bring fire into my eyes, tauten the muscles around them. Work against every feeling, greet A. enthusiastically if he comes by, happily tolerate B. in my room, and, despite pain and difficulty, draw in with long swallows everything that is said at C.'s.

But even when it turns out this way, with every mistake — and mistakes are inevitable — the whole thing, the easy and the difficult, will break down, and I will have to turn back into the circle.

Therefore, the best advice remains to accept everything, to act like a heavy mass even if you feel you are being blown away, to let no unnecessary step to be enticed from you, to regard others with the gaze of an animal, to feel no remorse, in short, to force down any remnants of this ghostly life, that is, to multiply the final quiet of the grave and to let nothing but this remain.

A characteristic motion in such a state is running your little finger over your eyebrows.

EXCURSION INTO THE MOUNTAINS

»I DON'T KNOW,« I CRIED without a sound, »I just don't know. If nobody comes, then nobody comes. I have not done anyone any harm, nobody has done me any harm, but nobody wants to help me. Absolutely nobody. But really it is not this way. Just that nobody helps me — otherwise absolutely nobody would be fine. I would really like — and why not? — to make an excursion in the company of absolutely nobody. Into the mountains of course, where else? How these nobodies press against each other, all these arms, crossed and entangled, all these feet, separated by tiny steps! It is understood that everyone is in tails. We don't walk so badly, and the wind moves through the gaps that we and our limbs leave open. In the mountains throats become free! It's a wonder we don't sing.«

THE BACHELOR'S MISFORTUNE

IT SEEMS SO AWFUL TO remain a bachelor, as an old man, hard pressed to preserve your dignity, to beg for acceptance when you would like to spend an evening with people, to be sick and be looking at the empty room for a week from the corner of your bed, always to say goodbye at the front door, never to rush up the stairs beside your wife, to have side doors in your room that lead only to other people's apartments, to carry your dinner home in your hand, to have to gaze at other people's children and not be allowed to continue saying: »I have none,« to model yourself in appearance and behavior after one or two bachelors from your memories of youth.

That is how it will be, except that in reality, today and later, you yourself will be standing there, with a body and a real head, and therefore also a forehead to beat with your hand.

THE MERCHANT

IT IS POSSIBLE THAT a few people pity me, but I don't notice. My small business fills me with concerns that make my forehead and temples ache, but without promising satisfaction in the future, because my business is small.

For hours in advance I must make decisions, keep awake the clerk from forgetting things, warn of feared mistakes, and in one season estimate the fashions of the next, not as they will appear among the people of my circle, but among the inaccessible people of the country.

Strangers have my money; their circumstances cannot be clear to me; I cannot imagine the misfortune that might strike them; how could I prevent it! Perhaps they have become wasteful and throw a party in a tavern garden and others delay their departure for America in order to spend a short time at this party.

When, on the evening of a working day, the business is closed and I suddenly see before me hours in which I will not be able to work to meet the incessant demands of my business, then my excitement, postponed in the morning, leaps within me like a returning flood. However, it is not restrained in me, and pulls me along without a destination.

And yet I cannot make use of this mood and can only go home, because my face and hands are dirty and sweaty, my jacket is spotted and dusty, the cap from my business is on my head and my boots are scratched up by the nails from the crates. I walk as though on waves, tap with the fingers of both hands and run them over the hair of approaching children.

But the walk is too short. Already I am in my building; I open the elevator door and step in.

Suddenly I realize that I am alone. Other people, who have to climb stairs, tire themselves out a little in the process, and have to wait, their lungs breathing rapidly, until someone comes to open the apartment door, and thus have a reason for anger and impatience; then they enter the antechamber, where they hang up their hats, and are alone only after they have walked through the hall, past a few glass doors and into their own rooms.

I, however, am alone as soon as I reach the

elevator, and, supported by my knees, look into the narrow mirror. When the elevator begins to rise, I say:

»Be still, step back, do you want to go into the shadows of the trees, behind the draperies of the windows, into the arboreal chamber?«

I speak with my teeth, and the bannisters glide down to the panes of frosted glass like rushing water.

»Fly away; your wings, which I have never seen, want to carry you to the rustic valley or to Paris, if you feel like going there.

Enjoy the view from the window when the processions come from every street, not avoiding each other, going through each other and allowing the square to be free again between their last rows. Wave with scarves, be shocked, be moved, praise the beautiful lady who passes by.

Go over the stream on the wooden bridge, nod to the children who are swimming, and be astonished at the hurrah of the thousand sailors on the distant battleship.

Pursue only the insignificant man, and when you have pushed him into a doorway, rob him and then watch, each with your hands in your pockets, how he sadly continues on his way in the street to the left.

The police, dispersed on their horses, restrain the animals and force you back. Let them; the empty streets will make them unhappy, I know it. As I said, they are already riding away in groups of two, slowly around the streetcorners, flying over the squares.«

Then I have to get out, let the elevator descend, and ring the doorbell. The girl opens the door as I greet her.

DISTRACTED OBSERVATION

WHAT WILL WE DO IN the spring days that are now rapidly approaching? This morning the sky was gray, but if you go to the window now, you are surprised and lean your cheek against the windowlatch.

Below you see the light of the setting sun on the face of the childish girl who is walking and looking around, and at the same time you see on her the shadow of the man behind her, who is walking faster.

Then the man has gone by and the child's face is covered in light.

THE WAY HOME

YOU SHOULD SEE THE persuasive power the air has after a thunderstorm! My virtues appear to me and overwhelm me, although I do not resist.

I march along and my tempo is the tempo of this side of the street, of this street, of this quarter. I am justly answerable for all the knocks on all the doors, on the tabletops, for all the toasts, for the lovers in their beds, in the scaffolding of the new buildings, pressed to the walls of houses in dark alleys, on the ottomans in the bordellos.

I compare my past with my future, but find both stupendous, can give neither my preference and can find fault only with the injustice of the providence that is favoring me in this way.

However, I am a little pensive when I enter my room, although nothing worthy of consideration has occurred to me while climbing the stairs. It is not much help to me that I open the window and that there is still music playing in a garden.

THE PEOPLE RUNNING BY

WHEN ONE IS TAKING a walk through the street at night, and a man — already visible from a distance because the street rises in front of us and the moon is full — runs toward us, we will not tackle him, even if he is weak and ragged, even if someone is running behind him and screaming, but we will let him continue running.

Because it is night, and we cannot do anything about the street's rising in front of us in the full moon, and besides, maybe these two have staged this chase for their own entertainment, maybe both of them are pursuing a third, maybe the first man is being pursued even though he is innocent, maybe the second man wants to kill him and we will become accomplices to the murder, maybe the two of them know nothing about one another and each is going independently to his bed, maybe they are sleepwalkers, maybe the first man is armed.

And after all, don't we have a right to be tired, haven't we drunk a lot of wine? We are happy when the second man has also vanished from sight.

THE PASSENGER

I STAND ON THE TRAM platform and am completely uncertain regarding my place in this world, in this city, in my family. I could not state even approximately which claims I could justifiably advance in any particular direction. I cannot defend the fact that I am standing on this platform, holding this loop, letting myself be carried by this tram, that people are avoiding the tram or walking silently or stopping in front of the store windows. — No one demands it of me, but this doesn't matter.

The tram approaches a stop, a girl takes a place near the steps, ready to get off. She appears as clearly to me as if I had touched her. She is dressed in black, the folds of her skirt hardly move, her blouse is tight and has a collar of fine white lace, she holds her left hand flat against the wall, the umbrella in her right hand is on the second to highest step. Her face is brown, her nose, slightly indented at the sides, ends broadly and roundly. She has a lot of brown hair and at her right temple the little hairs have been blown by the wind. Her little ear lies close to her head, but because I am standing close to her, I see the entire back of her right ear and the shadow at the root.

I asked myself then: How is it that she is not astonished with herself, that she keeps her mouth closed and says nothing?

CLOTHES

OFTEN WHEN I SEE clothes with various fringes, frills and pleats, which lie so beautifully over beautiful bodies, I think that they will not be preserved that way for long, but will get creases that can never be smoothed out, will gather dust that, thick in the embroidery, can never be removed, and that no woman would want to make herself so sad and ridiculous as to put on the same precious dress every morning and take it off in the evening.

And yet I see girls who are certainly pretty and who display many charming muscles and small bones and taut skin and masses of fine hair, and appear every day in this one natural mask, always laying the same face in the palms of the same hands and letting it be reflected in the mirror.

Only sometimes in the evening, when they arrive late from a party and see it in the mirror, does it appear threadbare, misshapen, dusty, already seen by everyone and hardly wearable anymore.

REJECTION

WHEN I MEET A BEAUTIFUL girl and ask her: »Be so good and come with me,« and she passes by without saying anything, what she means to say is this:

»You are no duke with a distinguished name, no broad American with an Indian physique, with a calm, level gaze, with skin massaged by the air of the prairies and the rivers that rush through them, you have made no journeys to the great seas or on them, wherever they are. So please tell me, why should a beautiful girl like me go with you?«

»You forget that no automobile carries you swaying through the streets with long thrusts; I do not see the gentlemen of your retinue, pressed into their clothes, murmuring benedictions to you as they walk behind you in a perfect half-circle; your breasts are well-arranged in your corset, but your hips and thighs compensate for that restraint; you are wearing a taffeta dress with pleats, such as delighted us so much last autumn, and yet you smile — this mortal danger on your body — from time to time.«

»Yes, we are both right, and in order not to make us both irrevocably aware of it we should — don't you think? — each go home alone.«

FOR AMATEUR JOCKEYS TO THINK ABOUT

NOTHING, WHEN ONE considers it, can tempt one to want to be first in a race.

When the orchestra strikes up, the glory of being recognized as the best rider of a particular country makes one so happy that it would be impossible to prevent remorse the next morning.

The envy of opponents, cunning, fairly influential people, must cause us suffering in the narrow winner's enclosure, through which we must now force ourselves on the way to the plain that only a short time before was empty before us except for a few riders whom we had already passed, small as they rode against the edge of the horizon.

Many of our friends hurry off to collect their winnings and only shout their hurrah to us over their shoulders, from the distant counters; the best friends, however, have bet nothing on our horse because they were afraid that if we had lost they would have been angry with us, but now, because our horse finished first and they have not won anything, they turn away when we go past and prefer to look along the grandstands.

The competitors behind us, firmly in their saddles, try to survey the misfortune that has befallen them and the injustice that has somehow been done to them; they assume a fresh appearance, as though a new race has to begin, a serious one after this child's game.

To many women the winner appears ridiculous because he puffs himself up and does not know what to do about the ceaseless handshaking, saluting, bowing and greeting from a distance. The losers, in contrast, have closed their mouths and are softly patting the necks of their horses, most of which are neighing.

Meanwhile the sky has become cloudy and now, in addition to all the rest, it starts to rain.

THE STREETWINDOW

WHOEVER LIVES ALONE and would still like to find human contact from time to time, whoever — with consideration for changes in the time of day, the weather, business affairs, and the like — wants to see some arm to which he could cling, — he will not be able to do this for long without a streetwindow. And even if he is not looking for anything at all and it is only as a tired man that he steps to the window-ledge, his eyes wandering between the people and the sky, and even if he does not want to and has tilted his head back slightly, the horses down below will pull him along in their wake of carriages and noise and finally into the concord of humanity.

THE WISH TO BECOME AN INDIAN

IF ONE ACTUALLY WERE an Indian, instantly ready, on the running horse, slanting into the air, trembling again and again over the trembling ground, until one shed the spurs, because there were no spurs, until one threw away the reins, because there were no reins, and hardly saw the land ahead as a smooth-mown heath, already without horse's neck and horse's head.

THE TREES

BECAUSE WE ARE LIKE tree trunks in the snow. They appear to lie smoothly, and with a small shove one should be able to push them away. No, it is impossible, because they are firmly bound to the earth. But see, even that is only appearance.

UNHAPPINESS

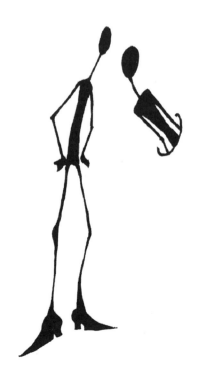

WHEN IT HAD ALREADY become unbearable — once toward evening in November — and I was running around the narrow carpet in my room like a race-track, horrified by the sight of the lit street, and turned again, and again found a new destination in the depths of the room, at the base of the mirror, and screamed, just to hear the scream that nothing answers and from which nothing takes the force of screaming, and which thus rises without a counter-weight, and cannot cease even when it falls silent — then the door opened from the wall, so quickly, because speed was necessary, and even the carriage horses down on the pavement reared up like horses that had become wild in battle and offered their throats.

In the form of a small ghost, a child emerged from the pitch-dark corridor, where no lamp was burning yet, and remained standing on the tips of its toes, on an imperceptibly shaking floorboard. Suddenly blinded by the twilight in the room, it tried to cover its face with its hands, but then unexpectedly calmed itself with a glance toward the window, where, in front of the crossbars, the ascending vapor from the streetlamps finally remained lying beneath the darkness. With its right elbow against the wall it held itself erect in front of the open door and let the draft from outside stroke its ankles as well as its throat and temples.

I took a quick look in its direction, said »Hello,« and, because I did not want to stand there half-naked, took my jacket from the fire screen. For a short time I held my mouth open in order to let the excitement escape. My eyelashes were trembling and I had a bad taste in my mouth; in short, this visit, which I had certainly been expecting, was the last thing I needed.

The child was still standing in the same place by the wall. It had pressed its right hand against the whitewashed surface of the wall and, with red cheeks, could not get enough of the wall's rough texture, which rubbed its fingertips. I said: »Is it really me you are looking for? It's not a mistake? There is nothing easier than to make a mistake in a large building like this. My name is Soandso, I live on the third floor. Am I the one you want to visit?«

»Be quiet!« the child said over its shoulder, »Everything is as it should be.«

»Then you should come into the room. I would like to close the door.«

»I just closed the door. Don't exert yourself. You should calm down.«

»Don't talk to me about exertion. Many people live on this hall, and of course I know all of them; most of them are coming home from work now; when they hear people speaking in a room, they feel they have the right to open the door and look to see what's happening. These people have their day's work behind them; why should they obey anyone in the evening, when they have a few hours of freedom? And besides, you know this yourself. Let me close the door.«

»What's wrong with you? What are you thinking? As far as I'm concerned everyone in the building can come in. And once again: I have already closed the door. Do you think you're the only one who can close it? I even locked it with the key.«

»That's good. I ask for nothing more. You didn't need to lock it. Now that you're here you should make yourself comfortable. You are my guest. Have complete trust in me. Don't be afraid. I will not force you to stay or go. Do I even need to say it? Do you know me so badly?«

»No. You really didn't need to say that. What's more, you shouldn't have said it. I'm a child; why are you making such a fuss over me?«

»It's not as bad as you make it out. Of course, a child. But you're not so small. You're already grown up. If you were a girl, you wouldn't be allowed to lock yourself up in a room with me like this.«

»We needn't worry about that. I just wanted to say that knowing you well does little to protect me; it only spares you the exertion of telling me lies. But still you compliment me. Stop it, please, stop it. What's more, I don't know you always and everywhere, especially in this darkness. It would be much better if you lit the lamp. No, it's better not to. Still, I won't forget that you've threatened me.«

»What? You say I threatened you? Please. In

fact I'm quite happy that you're finally here. I say
›finally‹ because it's already so late. I can't under-
stand why you've come so late. Perhaps because of
that I spoke so confusedly in my happiness that you
understood it as you did. I'll admit ten times over
that I spoke that way. Yes, I even threatened you
with everything you want. — Just no arguing, for
the love of God! — But how could you believe it?
How could you insult me like this? Why are you
doing everything in your power to ruin for me the
short time that you are here? A stranger would be
more accommodating than you.«

»I believe that; it wasn't anything profound. As
accommodating as a stranger could be to you I
already am by my very nature. You know it too, so
why this melancholy? Just tell me that you want to
joke around and I'll leave right away.«

»What? You dare to say even that to me? You're
a little too bold. In the end it's my room you're in.
You're rubbing your fingers against my wall like
crazy. My room, my wall! And besides, what you are
saying is ridiculous, not just brazen. You say that

your nature forces you to talk to me in this way. Really? Your nature forces you? That's very good of your nature. Your nature is mine, and when, in accordance with my nature, I am friendly to you, you should do the same.«

»Is that a friendly way to talk?«

»I'm talking about earlier.«

»Do you know how I'll be later?«

»I don't know anything.«

And I went to the night table and lit the candle. At that time I had neither gas nor electric light in my room. I sat at the table for a while, until I got tired of it, put on my overcoat, took my hat from the couch, and blew out the candle. On the way out I tripped over a chairleg.

On the stairs I met a tenant from the same floor.

»You're going out again, you rascal?« he asked, resting on his two legs, which were stretched out over two stairs.

»What should I do?« I said, »I just had a ghost in my room.«

»You say that with the same dissatisfaction you

would have if you had found a hair in your soup.«

»You're joking. But remember: a ghost is a ghost.«

»That's true. But what if one doesn't believe in ghosts?«

»And you think I believe in ghosts? But how does my disbelief help me?«

»It's very simple. You don't need to be afraid if a ghost comes to you.«

»Yes, but that's just the tangential fear. The real fear is the fear of what caused the apparition. And this fear doesn't go away. Right now there's an enormous amount of it in me.« Out of nervousness I began to go through all my pockets.

»But since the apparition itself didn't frighten you, you could have simply asked it why it was there.«

»You have obviously never spoken with any ghosts. One can never get clear information out of them. It's a pointless discussion. These ghosts seem to doubt their own existence more than we do, which is no surprise, considering their frailty.«

»But I've heard you can fatten them up.«

»You're right about that. It can be done. But who would do it?«

»Why not? If it were a female ghost, for example,« he said, and swung himself up to the next step.

»Aha,« I said, »but it is precisely in this case that it doesn't work.«

I reflected. My acquaintance was already so high up that in order to see me he had to bend forward under an arch in the stairwell. »All the same,« I called, »if you take away my ghost up there it's over between us forever.«

»But it was just a joke,« he said and pulled back his head.

»Then it's all right,« I said and could finally have gone for a walk. But because I felt so completely alone it seemed better to go back upstairs and lie down to sleep.

Contemplation

by Franz Kafka

originally published in German as *Betrachtung*
(Leipzig: Ernst Rowholt, 1913)

Translated by Kevin Blahut
Illustrations by Fedele Spadafora

Set in Janson

Published by Twisted Spoon Press
P.O. Box 21 — Preslova 12
150 21 Prague 5, Czech Republic
http://www.terminal.cz/~twispoon

Printed in the Czech Republic by Tiskárny Havlíčkův Brod

10 9 8 7 6 5 4 3 2